and the Sinister Smoke Ring

THE Berenstain BEAR SCOUTS
and the Sinister Smoke Ring

by Stan & Jan Berenstain
Illustrated by Michael Berenstain

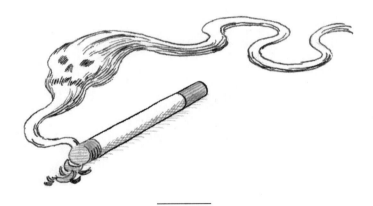

A
LITTLE APPLE
PAPERBACK

SCHOLASTIC INC.
New York Toronto London Auckland Sydney

ISBN 0-439-39753-7

12 11 10 9 8 7 6 5 4 3 2 1   7 8 9/9 0 1 2/0

Printed in the U.S.A.

First Scholastic printing, February 1997

• Table of Contents •

• Chapter 1 •

Ralph Is Ready to Roll

Ralph Ripoff was pacing in nervous circles around the main cabin of the rundown houseboat he called home. Watching Ralph go around in circles made Squawk, his pet parrot, nervous.

"Round he goes! Round he goes!" squawked Squawk, shifting and bobbing on his perch. "And where he stops, no one knows! Round he goes! Round —"

"Shut up, birdbrain!" snarled Ralph.

Squawk ducked in case Ralph threw something at him. But Ralph had heard the sound he'd been waiting for and was

out the door and down the gangplank. It was the little "klunk" the mailbear made when he raised the red flag on Ralph's mailbox.

Ralph lowered the flag and took out a handful of mail, which included a folded-up newspaper. He was back inside like a shot and seated in his messy corner "office," reading the latest issue of his favorite newspaper, *The Bear Street Journal.*

He found what he was looking for on page three. It was a small story headlined "Moose Tobacco Has Huge Loss." It went on to say, "The Moose Company, manufacturer of Moose Cigarettes and other tobacco products, had its third loss in as many quarters." It was a bit of news Ralph had been waiting for.

"Ralph," he said, addressing his favorite person in all the world, "we're ready to roll." With that, he took a piece of his fancy business stationery and rolled it into his typewriter. Clack-clack-clack-clack-clack-ding! went the typewriter.

"Clack-clack-clack-clack-clack-ding!" said Squawk, who was just as good at sound effects as he was at fresh remarks.

Ralph winged a pillow at Squawk and missed. Ralph was writing an important business letter and he didn't want to be distracted. It was part of a plan he had been working on for some time. This is how the letter started:

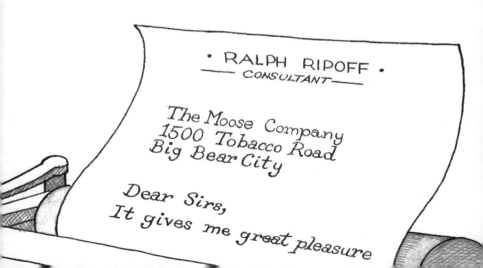

• Chapter 2 •

One of Our Scouts Is Missing

Sister couldn't quite figure out what had gotten into Brother. But whatever it was, it worried her.

It wasn't as though he was turning into a monster before her very eyes. But *something* was going on, and she didn't know what to make of it. Brother was normally friendly and pleasant. But lately he'd turned mean and surly. Normally, Brother was full of plans for scouting projects. But lately scouting seemed the furthest thing from his mind.

And was it possible? Was Brother beginning to talk out of the side of his mouth and walk with a swagger? There was no question about it. Somewhere along the way, Brother's straight arrow had gotten a little bent.

The worst of it was that he was beginning to remind her of someone. But she couldn't for the life of her think who it was.

And now this. The troop was gathered in their secret chicken coop clubhouse for an important merit-badge meeting, and Brother was missing.

"Where do you suppose he is?" said Fred.

Sister shrugged.

"He knows we can't choose our next merit badge without him," said Lizzy. "Because all merit-badge votes have to be unanimous."

Sister shrugged again. Fred and Lizzy were annoyed with Brother. Sister was more worried than annoyed. Who *was* it that Brother was reminding her of? It was on the tip of her mind. But she just couldn't quite think who it was. Was it somebody from TV or the movies? Or was it somebody from real life?

"Maybe he's just late," said Fred. "It's basketball season, and you know how he is about basketball. Maybe he got into a game and lost track of the time."

Fred went to a window and looked out. There was no sign of Brother. He opened the window and leaned out for a better look. There was still no sign of Brother.

"What's that smell?" said Lizzy. Along with her super eyesight and her extraspecial hearing, Lizzy had an uncanny sense of smell.

That's the way it was with the "one for all, and all for one" Bear Scouts. One of the reasons they were such a great team was that each member brought something special to the troop. Straight-arrow Brother was a natural leader. Spunky Sister was all nerve. Supersmart Fred read

the dictionary and the encyclopedia just for fun. Lizzy was so in tune with nature that she could see a fawn in a thicket, count the petals of a daisy in a single glance, and smell a rose a half mile away.

"I don't smell anything," said Fred.

"Neither do I," said Sister.

"Hmm," said Lizzy, sniffing the air. "It's something I've smelled before."

"Hey," said Fred, looking across the field. "There's some kind of ruckus going on behind Farmer Ben's barn over near the road."

"Look!" said Sister. "A bunch of folks marching around carrying signs."

"And there's Farmer Ben in the middle," added Fred, "jumping up and down and waving a pitchfork. Come on. Let's get over there and see what's up."

Fred and Sister headed for the clubhouse's secret hollow-tree exit, but Lizzy hung back. "It's tobacco," she said. "That's what it is, tobacco. My Uncle Walt used to smoke a pipe, and that's what it smelled like."

Sister stopped dead in her tracks. The hard stare, the tough-guy swagger, and now Lizzy's mention of tobacco had put the puzzle together. It was Too-Tall Grizzly, leader of the Too-Tall gang, that Brother was reminding her of. Too-Tall and his gang were the worst. Not only were they thieves and bullies, they had been suspended six times for smoking!

Was it possible that straight-arrow Brother was hanging around with Too-Tall? Was it possible that he was thinking of joining the gang?

Fred and Lizzy were on their way to the ruckus. Sister had to hurry to catch up.

• Chapter 3 •
As the Crow Flies

About a mile from the scouts' secret clubhouse as the crow flies, across the railroad tracks, in the scruffy woods north of the auto graveyard, was the secret headquarters of the Too-Tall gang. The crow, or anyone else happening by, would be well advised not to enter that scruffy woods but just to keep on going. Because the headquarters of the Too-Tall gang was not only secret, it was dangerous. Cubs who had been brave or foolish enough to ignore the "Keep Out" signs tended to come out of the woods minus their lunch money, their watches, and, if the gang was in a playful mood, their trousers.

But Brother was too busy playing basketball to notice trousers in trees or the fact that all the members of the Too-Tall gang were sporting spiffy-looking watches.

The scruffy woods echoed with the thump-thump-thump of a hard-fought basketball game. It was a half-court, two-against-three game, with Brother and Too-Tall against Vinnie, Skuzz, and Smirk. They were all good players. But

KEEP OUT!

Brother was a really wizard point guard. He was a good shooter, a great dribbler, and he could run all day.

Brother drove to the basket, dribbled behind his back, but, instead of going in for a lay up, passed off to Too-Tall, who swished a ten-foot jumper.

"Time-out!" shouted Vinnie, who was badly out of breath. In fact, they were all gasping for breath, except for Brother, who was breathing easily.

"Smoke, if you got 'em," said Too-Tall.

All the gang members except Too-Tall took singles out of their shirt pockets and lit up. Too-Tall had a whole pack.

"Have a coffin nail," said Too-Tall, offering Brother a cigarette.

"Coffin nail?" said Brother.

"It's a gag," said Too-Tall. "You know, it's what goody-goodies say about cigarettes."

Brother had never even tried to smoke and wasn't eager to. "Well, isn't it true," he said, "about smoking being bad for your health?"

"Hey!" said Too-Tall. "Ya wanna live forever?"

"What's a matter?" said Skuzz. "Are ya chicken?"

"Ya wanna join the gang or not?" said Vinnie.

"You mean you want me to join the gang?" said Brother.

"What d'ya think you're doing here, you dumb jerk?" said Smirk.

"Watch your mouth, creep!" snarled Too-Tall. Smirk backed off.

"Brother's a cool cub," continued Too-Tall. "I've had my eye on him for a while. Not only does he play good hoops, he's a stand-up guy. He's got guts. Look how he stood up to us when we bothered his little scout friends."

Brother reached over and took a cigarette from the pack. Too-Tall held out his lighter.

"Hey, that lighter is really cool," said Brother. "Where'd you get it?"

"Picked it up at Biff Bruin's Pharmacy," said Too-Tall, snapping on the flame.

"What do you mean, 'picked it up'?" asked Brother.

"Just what I said. The gang put on a fake fight, and I picked it up."

There was no mistaking Too-Tall's meaning. He'd *stolen* the cigarette lighter. The thought brought back all the bad things Brother had heard about the Too-Tall gang.

But sitting there in front of the gang's fantastic clubhouse — it was made out of old car parts and made the Bear Scout chicken coop clubhouse look like — well, a chicken coop — the bad things faded into the background. Brother felt as if he were sitting on top of the world. The fact that it was the top of the underworld didn't seem to matter.

Too-Tall lit Brother's cigarette, and for a while Brother tried to keep from choking.

• Chapter 4 •

Legal Crop versus Filthy Weed

Lizzy's uncanny sense of smell was right, as usual. Farmer Ben was standing in the middle of a patch of carefully tended dark-green plants, yelling and waving his pitch-fork. He was furious.

DOWN WITH TOBACCO! SMOKING KILLS!

BAN SMOK WE'RE N(JOKING

"Dang protesters!" he shouted. "Get off my property, you dang busybodies. Tobacco is a legal crop. What I grow on my own property is my business!"

The protesters were just as angry. They marched around Ben's tobacco patch, thrusting their signs up and down and chanting, "Down with tobacco! Smoking kills!" Their signs said things like BAN SMOKING! WE'RE NOT JOKING!, SMOKING KILLS THOUSANDS!, and TOBACCO IS A FILTHY WEED! Though they were marching mostly on the road, they had to go on Ben's property to circle the tobacco patch.

"Look!" said Sister.

The scouts looked and recognized one of the protesters. It was none other than their old "friend" Miss Stickler. She was the one who substituted for Scout Leader Jane when Jane ran for mayor. Miss Stickler had more than lived up to her name when she filled in for Jane. She was a stickler for just about anything you could think of: saying "who" when you should say "whom," dotting your "i's" with little circles, slouching — just about anything.

When the scouts saw her, they automatically straightened their hats and neckerchiefs.

"Well, as I live and breathe," said Miss Stickler. "It's the Bear Scouts come to join our crusade! But aren't you one scout short?"

"Crusade?" said Fred.

"Yes," said Miss Stickler. "The crusade against tobacco and the evils of smoking!"

"Don't you dare join these busybodies," said Ben.

The scouts were in an awkward position. They knew that smoking was very bad for your health. But Farmer Ben was a friend of theirs. After all, it was Ben who let them convert his old chicken coop into a clubhouse.

But the scouts didn't have to choose sides. Because that's when Chief Bruno and Officer Marguerite arrived in the police car, lights flashing and siren screaming.

• Chapter 5 •

Chief Bruno Lays Down the Law

You'd have thought that Farmer Ben and
the protesters would have stopped shouting when the police arrived. But they
didn't. They just stopped shouting at each
other and started shouting at Chief Bruno
and Officer Marguerite instead.

"Arrest them, Chief!" shouted Ben.
"They're trespassin'! Tobacco is a legal
crop, and they have no right to picket my
property!"

"Don't you dare, Bert Bruno!" said Miss
Stickler. "Farmer Ben is a disgrace to agri-
culture, growing that filthy weed. We're

going to protest and protest and protest, and there's nothing you can do about it!"

"Oh, yeah? How would you like a taste of this?" said Ben, waving the pitchfork under her nose.

"Just you try it! You filthy tobacco grower!" cried Miss Stickler, her eyes flashing and her dangle earrings dangling. "On with the march, ladies!"

Miss Stickler and her group started marching and chanting again. "Down with tobacco! Smoking kills! Down with tobacco! Smoking kills!" It wasn't until the chief blew an ear-piercing blast on his police whistle that both sides quieted down.

"Now just hush! Just calm down and let me explain something to you!" said the

chief. "You're both right, and you're both wrong!"

He turned to Ben. "Ben, you're right about one thing. They may not come onto your property. That's trespassing. But if they stay on the road, they can protest all they want. It's called freedom of speech."

He turned to the protesters. "Miss Stickler, you and your protesters are right about tobacco and smoking. It causes death and disease. No question about it. But it's a legal crop, and Ben has every right to grow it if he chooses to!"

Chief Bruno's explanation pleased no one.

"You're just siding with them because you used to be in Miss Stickler's class!" complained Ben.

"And I say you're siding with this tobacco grower because you're probably a smoker yourself!" accused Miss Stickler. "It seems to me I caught you smoking when you were in middle school."

"That's right, Miss Stickler," said the chief. "You did, indeed. But I'm happy to report that I haven't smoked since."

"Humph," humphed Miss Stickler.

Chief Bruno was losing patience. "All right, folks. Here's the deal. I'm going to leave Officer Marguerite here to keep the peace. She has a cell phone, and if there's any more trespassing or threatening with a pitchfork, she's going to call for the paddy wagon and take you all in. Is that understood?"

Farmer Ben growled under his breath and put down the pitchfork.

"We've made our point for now," said Miss Stickler. "Come, ladies, and bring your signs." The group headed down the road to where Miss Stickler had parked her van. "Oh, yes, scouts. I have a message for you from Scout Leader Jane. She knew I would be over here today. She said if I saw you to tell you that tomorrow's Bear Scout meeting will be at three o'clock in

Dr. Gert's office in Beartown Hospital. She'll also be leaving messages for you at home."

Then Miss Stickler and her antismoking protesters piled into her van.

"Scout meeting at the hospital?" said Sister.

"What's it about?" said Fred.

But Miss Stickler, who drove like a demon, was off with a roar and a cloud of dust.

• Chapter 6 •

A Problem with Brother

"A Saturday scout meeting at the hospital instead of at Scout Leader Jane's
house," said Fred.

"What do you suppose it's about?" said
Sister. "It must be something pretty important."

"It must be," agreed Fred. "So Brother
better be there."

Sister sighed. "I'm afraid we have a
problem with Brother."

Fred and Lizzy looked hard at Sister.
"You know where he was today, don't you?"
said Fred.

"I'm not sure, but I think he was hanging out with the Too-Tall gang."

"Hanging out with the Too-Tall gang?" chorused Fred and Lizzy. They couldn't have been more shocked if Sister had told them Brother had sprouted horns and a tail.

"They're a bunch of bullies and thugs!" said Fred.

"They don't study the three R's at school. They study the three S's: stealing, smoking, and scrapping," said Lizzy.

"They're the lowest of the low," said Fred.

"They might be the lowest of the low," said Sister, "but they're pretty high-and-mighty around the schoolyard."

"Yeah," admitted Fred. "Especially since they formed that rap group and won the mayor's talent show."

THEY'RE THE LOWEST OF THE LOW.

"I heard they may even cut a record," said Lizzy.

"Maybe it's just basketball," said Fred, trying to look at the bright side. "Too-Tall's always after Brother to play basketball."

"Maybe Brother's just flattered," said Lizzy.

"'Maybe' isn't going to get Brother to that big meeting at the hospital tomorrow," said Sister.

"Gee, what are you going to do?" asked Fred.

"I don't know what I'm going to do," said Sister. "But I'll figure out something."

The scouts had been heading home. "Look," said Sister. "The big hospital meeting is tomorrow afternoon. Let's meet here at Eagle Road at nine o'clock tomorrow morning. And I'll let you know whether Mr. Straight-Arrow Nice-Guy Brother has turned into a no-good jerk."

The threesome parted company and headed for their homes.

• Chapter 7 •
Suspicions Confirmed

Fred and Lizzy were waiting the next morning on Eagle Road. Sister showed up at nine o'clock sharp.

"I've got bad news, worse news, and worst news," said Sister. "The bad news is that he's definitely been hanging out with Too-Tall."

"How do you know?" asked Fred.

"It's obvious," said Sister. "He's been acting more and more like Too-Tall for a couple of days. You know, talking out of the side of his mouth, acting tough, throwing his weight around. And last night I caught him practicing Too-Tall poses in front of the mirror. It's a clear case of hero worship."

Fred and Lizzy looked glum. "Okay, what's the worse news?" asked Lizzy.

"The worse news is that he's not only hanging out with the Too-Tall gang, he's smoking with them."

"Hoo-ee!" said Lizzy.

"Guh!" said Fred.

They both looked as if they'd been punched in the belly. Acting tough was one thing. Hanging out was another. But smoking was a whole different thing.

"Was there a big blowup when you told him you knew?" asked Fred.

"I didn't tell him I knew," said Sister. "I didn't have to. I could smell cigarette smoke on his clothes."

"Didn't your parents smell it?" asked Lizzy.

"Nope," said Sister. "He got out of his clothes as soon as he got home and took a shower. Said he was sweaty from playing

basketball."

"Maybe he *was* sweaty from playing basketball," said Fred.

"Look," said Sister. "I may not have a super sniffer like Lizzy, but I can tell sweat from cigarette smoke."

"But the Too-Tall gang smokes like a chimney," said Lizzy. "Maybe it was just from being around them."

"Which brings me to the worst news." She took something out of her pocket and held it up. It was a cigarette. "I found this in his shirt pocket."

Fred and Lizzy stared at it. It looked like a stick of dynamite that could blow the Bear Scouts apart.

"Come on. There's no time to lose," said Sister. "We've got to see somebody."

"Who?" said Fred.

"The person we always go to when we've got big trouble."

The Bear Scouts, minus one, headed for town.

Since it was Saturday morning, Gramps was in his usual place in the little park at the center of Beartown. He was on his regular bench in the shade of Old Shag, the great historic tree (and backscratcher) that he and his good friends the Bear Scouts had recently saved from the chain-saw and the crooked schemes of Ralph Ripoff and his crony Mayor Honeypot.

But that was then and this was now, and Gramps was sitting on his favorite bench relaxing, reading the newspaper. He wasn't expecting the scouts. But he was glad to see them coming along the path. But the usually smiling scouts looked glum, and they were one scout short.

"Well," said Gramps. "If it isn't Bear Country's most important uniformed group after the army and navy."

"Hi, Gramps," said Sister. "I'm afraid we've got a serious problem."

"I'm sorry to hear that," said Gramps. "But I'll be happy to help in any way I can. By the way — where's Brother?"

"He's our serious problem," said Fred.

"Oh?" said Gramps. "Why don't you climb up here and tell me the whole story."

That's what they did. Sister, Fred, and Lizzy pitched in and told Gramps the shocking story of Brother's downfall. They told about the missed merit-badge meeting, the tough-guy attitude, the Too-Tall connection, the cigarette smell, the quick shower, and the cigarette in the shirt pocket.

Gramps didn't interrupt or try to hurry the story the way some grown-ups do when cubs are telling them something. He just listened.

The scouts finished their story and waited for Gramps to say something. But he just sat there with that look older folks get when they're thinking about something that happened to them long ago.

"You know, I used to smoke," said Gramps.

"You did?" said Fred.

"Gee!" said Lizzy.

"But you don't smoke now," said Sister.

"Nope," said Gramps.

"How come you smoked?" asked Fred.

Gramps grinned. "I think that's a story I'd better save for Brother. I think he may find it very interesting. Tell me something. Where do you think I might run into Brother today?"

"He took off early this morning," said Sister. "As he was leaving, I yelled to him about today's three o'clock meeting at the hospital. But I'm not even sure he heard me. I'm pretty sure he was heading for Too-Tall's place behind the auto graveyard. But he's supposed to get back and do some errands today."

Gramps folded his newspaper, stood up, and stretched. "Well," he said, "I'd better get a move on if I'm going to run into Brother accidentally on purpose."

• Chapter 8 •

A Port in the Storm

"What d'ya mean, he's gotta go home and do some errands?" said Skuzz. "What're we runnin' here, a sewing circle? I say he's gotta stay here and start his initiation!"

"*You* say? *You* say?" said Too-Tall. He towered over Skuzz. "You must be lookin' for a smack in the mouth!"

Skuzz was big and very tough. But there was no way he was going to stand up to Too-Tall. "I don't get it," he mumbled. "Letting some goody-goody into the gang just because he can dribble." He slunk away and sat in one of the stolen car seats in front of the car parts clubhouse. He took out a cigarette and lit up.

"Come on," said Too-Tall. "I'll walk you to the edge of the woods. And don't worry about Skuzz. He needs to be slapped down once in a while. But be sure you're back here this afternoon to start your initiation into the gang. Well, so long. Keep loose." Too-Tall headed back into the woods.

Initiation! thought Brother as he walked along the old dirt road past the auto graveyard. He hadn't counted on an

initiation. And even though Too-Tall was excusing him from some of the worst parts, like beating up somebody, breaking windows, and setting off stink bombs, he was still going to have to do some stuff, like smoke ten cigarettes in less than an hour and steal some car parts for the club-house.

There was more to hanging out with Too-Tall than basketball. A lot more. But Brother was still excited about being around the Too-Tall gang. It was almost as if they were celebrities. Especially Too-Tall. And when he was with them, he felt like one, too. So what if he had to smoke a few cigarettes. Being part of the Too-Tall gang was like being king of the hill with-out having to climb the hill.

As Brother walked along beside the auto graveyard trying to convince himself that the Too-Tall gang wasn't all that bad, he saw a familiar person poking around among the car wrecks. It was Gramps. His pickup truck was parked nearby.

"Hey, Gramps," he called. "What are you doing here?"

"Hello, Brother," said Gramps. "Looking for parts for my trusty old pickup. I could use an extra tailpipe and maybe a backup fuel pump. How about you?"

"Just playing some hoops back there in the woods," said Brother.

"I'll be heading home," said Gramps.

"Me too," said Brother.

"Can I give you a lift?" said Gramps, heading toward the pickup.

"Sure thing," said Brother. He saw Gramps all the time. But he had never been so glad to see him as he was this very moment!

Seeing Gramps and his friendly old pickup was almost like finding a port in a storm. It reminded him of an experience he'd had when he was really little —

maybe about three years old. He'd been looking for pretty stones and followed a little stream into a nearby woods. He remembered how exciting it was when he followed it into a dark woods. But mostly he remembered how scary it was when he got turned around and thought he was lost. But then he climbed a little hill and saw his very own house and yard just beyond the woods. What a relief!

"Wasn't that Too-Tall I saw you with back there?" said Gramps. "Pretty fast company."

"I guess so," said Brother.

"It's funny how history repeats itself," said Gramps. "You know, until the Too-Tall gang came along, the Burnt House gang held the record for getting suspended. That was my gang."

"You were in a gang?" said Brother.

"Sure was," said Gramps. "We used to meet in an old burnt house. That's where we got our name. The old burnt house smelled so bad from smoke that nobody could tell we'd been smoking."

"You used to smoke?" said Brother.

"We were smoking fools," said Gramps.

"But you don't smoke now," said Brother. "You must have given it up."

"Sure did," said Gramps.

After crossing the railroad tracks, Gramps drove up the winding road into the hill section. It was a pretty area. But it certainly wasn't the way home. But Brother didn't mind. The errands he was supposed to do weren't urgent. He'd just told Too-Tall that.

But he was beginning to wonder where Gramps was headed.

• Chapter 9 •

Gramps Remembers

"Who all was in your gang?" asked Brother.

"Oh, it wasn't *my* gang," said Gramps. "They just sort of joined me up the way, I'd guess, the Too-Tall gang is trying to join you up. Now, let's see. The leader was Willy Gavel. Boy, talk about tough!"

"You mean *Judge* Gavel? Judge *William* Gavel?" said Brother.

"One and the same," said Gramps. "And there was Amos Toll."

"Toll's Hardware," said Brother.

"That's right," said Gramps. "The funny

thing is we've stayed friends all these years. We go fishing together, play cards."

They were driving along Hill Road. Brother thought he knew his way around, but he'd never been up this way before.

"What happened to the Burnt House gang?" asked Brother.

"Oh, things happened and the gang sort of broke up," said Gramps.

"What kind of things?" said Brother.

"The usual," said Gramps. "Too many suspensions, too many fights, too many broken windows. Getting caught with cigarettes." Gramps was slowing down. "Say,

YOU MEAN JUDGE GAVEL? JUDGE WILLIAM GAVEL?

how would you like to meet a couple of my old gang-member friends?"

"Okay," said Brother.

Gramps pulled to a stop. They got out of the pickup. Gramps led Brother along a winding path.

Brother looked around. "Hey!" he said. "This is a cemetery!"

"That's right," said Gramps. "And there're my two friends, Ben Bearson and Grant Grizzwood, right over there. See? They're buried near each other."

Brother stared at the two gravestones. One said, "Here lies Ben Bearson, husband and father." The other said, "Here lies Grant Grizzwood, beloved husband."

"Grant and his Mrs. never had any cubs," said Gramps. "I stopped smoking when the gang broke up. Willie and Amos smoked for quite a while. But they finally managed to quit. These two fellows stayed with it, and that's what killed them. It's addictive, you know. It's pretty hard to quit once you're hooked."

It was a large cemetery. There were gravestones as far as the eye could see.

"I daresay," said Gramps, "that cigarettes put a lot of these folks in their graves. Maybe as many as half. Well, let's head back. What do you say we stop off at the Burger Bear for some lunch?"

Brother didn't answer right away. "That'll be fine, Gramps," he said.

"And then," said Gramps, "I understand you've got some kind of scout meeting at the hospital."

"At three o'clock," said Brother.

• Chapter 10 •

"Wrong, Tobacco Breath!"

The first thing Sister, Fred, and Lizzy noted as they approached the hospital was that Brother was not there. So much for getting Brother back on the straight and narrow. If Gramps couldn't turn him around, nobody could. But there was no use brooding about it. Up the hospital steps they went.

"You mean Dr. Gert is boss of this whole hospital?" said Sister as the scouts climbed the front steps.

"I guess so," said Fred. "It says so on that sign on the hospital lawn."

The sign told about a big antismoking health rally the hospital was planning. At the bottom it said, "Dr. Gert Grizzly, Director."

"Boy," said Fred. "You can see the whole downtown from up here."

"Look," said Sister. "Isn't that Ralph Ripoff going into the Grizzly Arms Motel?"

"It sure is, and he's carrying some kind of case," said Lizzy. "I wonder what he's up to."

"No good," said Sister. "You can count on that."

"They'd better lock up their towels and shampoo," said Fred. "Half the stuff in that houseboat of his is stolen."

"Whatever Ralph's up to, it's got nothing to do with us," said Sister.

They were just about to enter the lobby when who should pull up in front but Gramps. And who should climb out of the pickup and come running up the hospital steps but Brother. Hallelujah!

Sister was wrong about Ralph. He was after much bigger game than towels and shampoo. He was after the biggest, fattest deal of his whole crooked career.

"Could you direct me to the Moose meeting?" said Ralph to the desk clerk.

The clerk eyed him with suspicion. Ralph's reputation for stealing anything that wasn't nailed down was well known. "Conference Room B, sir. Just down the hall."

As Ralph moved along the carpeted hall, he rechecked the names of the Moose

COULD YOU DIRECT ME TO THE MOOSE MEETING?

executives. "Hmm — Wheeze, Tarr, and McSnuff," he murmured. He found the door marked B and entered.

"Messieurs Wheeze, Tarr, and McSnuff, I presume," said Ralph. "The savior of Moose Tobacco, at your service."

Ralph went right to work setting up his easel and flip chart.

"Just a minute, please," said one of the three who were seated at the conference table. "I'm Mr. Wheeze, Chairman of Moose Tobacco. This is Mr. Tarr, President, and Mr. McSnuff, Vice President. And we demand to know if you are the person who wrote this letter!" He thrust the letter at Ralph.

Ralph read it aloud: "'Dear Sirs, This is to inform you that I am prepared to save Moose Tobacco, to turn it from a pitiful failure into a rip-roaring, moneymaking success. Just present yourselves at the Grizzly Arms Motel . . .' Yes, I wrote that letter. But let's get down to business. We'll play a little Q and A for starters. Question one: Just what is it your company sells?"

The three executives looked puzzled.

"Why, we sell cigarettes and other tobacco products, of course," said Mr. Wheeze.

"Wrong, Tobacco Breath!" shouted Ralph, opening his presentation to the first page. Three words were printed on it in big block letters. "You're not selling cigarettes," he said, pointing to the words one by one. "You're selling *Excitement! Adventure! Sophistication!*

"Question two!" said Ralph, turning to the next page. It showed a gloomy-looking moose standing in a pond, eating some droopy water plants. "What's this?"

"It's our trademark, of course," said Mr. Tarr. "Our hundred-year-old trademark that appears on every pack of Moose Cigarettes."

"Wrong again!" cried Ralph. "It's your *former* trademark." He turned the page. "*This* is your exciting, daring, sophisticated *new* trademark!"

"Very interesting, Mr. Ripoff," said Mr. Wheeze. "Very interesting indeed. Please tell us more."

Ralph told them more — a whole lot more. He told them about the cool Moe Moose jackets, caps, vests, and backpacks smokers would get by sending in empty Moose Cigarette packs. He told them about the fabulous Moe Moose rock concerts that Moose Cigarettes would sponsor. He told them that the name Moe Moose would be on everyone's lips — not to mention Moose Cigarettes.

And, best of all, he told them about Project X, a project so secret that Ralph looked both ways before revealing it, even though there was no one else in the room but the three Moose executives, and the door was closed.

The three executives went wide-eyed with awe and excitement as they took in the size and scope of Project X. They did not even quibble when Ralph referred to it as the Eighth Wonder of the World.

Excitement and optimism filled Conference Room B. Moe Moose would be a sensation. Moose Tobacco would make a fortune.

There was only one note of caution in Conference Room B that day. It was sounded by Vice President McSnuff. He wondered if perhaps with all the cool clothes and rock concerts and such, it might seem that Moose Tobacco was trying to sell cigarettes to cubs.

"Ridiculous!" shouted Mr. Wheeze.

"Impossible!" roared Mr. Tarr.

Ralph agreed. "There is no way folks could think that," he said. "Because everybody knows that selling cigarettes to cubs is *illegal.*"

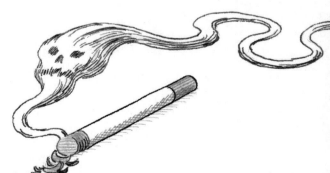

• Chapter 11 •
A Definition of Cool

Scout Leader Jane was waiting in the hospital lobby. She gathered the scouts and guided them to the elevator.

"Now, I realize," she said, "you've already given a lot of thought to your next merit badge. But just this once I want to choose. I want you to go for the Public Health Merit Badge. It's important. That's what this meeting with Dr. Gert is about."

Sister, Fred, and Lizzy looked at each other. The only thing they'd given a lot of thought to was *Brother's* personal health. Brother stared straight ahead.

Dr. Gert was waiting for them on the sixth floor. "Thank you for bringing the scouts, Jane. Come, let's go to my office."

They passed through a sort of picture gallery on the way.

"What are all these pictures?" asked Sister.

"This is my Horrors of Smoking exhibition," said Dr. Gert. "I show it to patients to get them to stop smoking."

"Does it work?" asked Fred.

"Not as often as I'd like," said the doctor.

"Wow!" said Sister. "That one looks like the bottom of a coal mine."

"The bottom of a coal mine is a healthier place," said Dr. Gert. "That happens to be the lung of someone who smoked a pack a day for twenty years. Anyway, come into my office. That's part of what I want to talk to you about.

"But first," said Dr. Gert as they entered, "did you notice the sign in front of the hospital — the one about the big anti-smoking health rally we're planning?"

"Sure," said Sister. "What's it going to be like?"

"It's still in the planning stage," said Dr. Gert. "It'll be about the dangers of smoking — how smoking affects the lungs, the heart, and just about every other part of the body. We'll have free blood-pressure checks, we'll check lungs, we'll have treadmills to test heart rates — that sort of thing. How does it sound?"

The scouts were silent.

"That bad?" said Dr. Gert with a smile.

"It sounds okay for grown-ups," said Fred. "But I don't think it'll go over that well with cubs."

"What *would* go over with cubs?" asked Dr. Gert.

"Some kind of a show with lots of action," said Sister. "You know, with balloons and stuff. Some kind of contest with prizes."

"I know a lot about doctoring," said Dr. Gert. "But I don't know much about putting on a show."

"We know someone who does!" said Fred. "Ralph Ripoff is a genius at putting on shows. He's the one that put on the big Pizza Shack grand opening."

"Yes," said Dr. Gert, "but isn't Mr. Ripoff a rather shady character?"

"As shady as they come," said Lizzy. "But he's kind of a friend of ours. He might enjoy doing something decent for a change."

"Hmm, let me think about that," said Dr. Gert. "But let's get down to business. I want our rally to make a really strong 'don't start smoking' statement to cubs. I want your advice on that. What about including my Horrors of Smoking exhibition? Do you think that would persuade cubs not to start smoking?"

"You'd think so," said Fred. "But lots of cubs think it's cool to do dangerous things. I know it sounds dumb. But some cubs are like that."

"What about how smoking gives you bad breath?" said Dr. Gert. "Would that discourage cubs from smoking?"

"It might do some good with middle-schoolers who are into kissing and stuff," said Sister. "But younger cubs are pretty gross about smells — especially boys."

"How about lecturing them?" said Dr. Gert, beginning to get a little frustrated. "Just telling them not to smoke or else?"

"It'll work on cubs like us," said Fred, "who aren't going to smoke in the first place."

"All right, that's you," said Dr. Gert. "But how about the cubs that do? Why do *they* smoke? You've been remarkably quiet, Brother. What do *you* think?"

"I guess it's mostly because they think it's cool," said Brother.

"Cool," said Dr. Gert. "That's a word I hear often. Exactly what does it mean?"

"That's a good question," said Brother.

"How about giving me a good answer," said Dr. Gert.

"'Cool' is a whole lot of stuff put together," said Brother.

"Yeah," said Sister. "Like pretending you don't care what anybody else thinks."

"And doing stuff because grown-ups say you shouldn't," said Lizzy.

"And trying to act older than you are," said Fred.

"I guess peer pressure's a big part of it," said Brother, blushing a little. "Trying to make other cubs think you're cool."

"I guess we're not such hot consultants," said Fred.

"You're doing fine," said Dr. Gert. "Just keep thinking about it. Maybe you'll come up with something. Meanwhile, I've been thinking about your Mr. Ripoff. I think we need him. Go see if you can talk him into helping us out."

• Chapter 12 •

The Weight of the World

"Come on," said Fred as the cubs went down the hospital's front steps. "If we hurry we can catch him there."

"Catch who where?" asked Lizzy.

"Catch Ralph at the Grizzly Arms Motel," said Fred. "Don't you remember? We saw him going in there."

"Sure," said Lizzy. "But that was quite a while ago."

"It's worth a try," said Sister. "It'll save us a trip to his houseboat." Ralph's houseboat was moored in a backwater of Great

Roaring River way over past Farmer Ben's farm.

"Is there anything I can do for you cubs?" asked the motel desk clerk.

"Yes," said Fred. "Do you remember that fellow that came in here a while ago? The one wearing the straw hat and the green suit? Is he still here?"

"Don't forget the cane and the spats," whispered Sister.

"How could I forget," said the clerk. "No, he's long gone."

"Thank you," said Fred.

The scouts left the motel and headed home.

The scouts were quiet as they walked through town. Past the Burger Bear, past the Pizza Shack, past Biff Bruin's Pharmacy. All of which sold cigarettes. There was even a cigarette machine in front of Biff Bruin's Pharmacy.

The scouts had come all the way through town without speaking a single word. That was an awfully long spell of being thoughtful and quiet. Sister decided to break the spell. "Okay, gang!" she yelled. "Last one to Eagle Road is a rotten egg!"

Off they went in a cloud of dust, running as if their lives depended on it. Running to get out from under the weight of the world. At least the part of it that had to do with smoking.

• Chapter 13 •

Brother's Big Idea

Brother woke up the next morning feeling like a new cub. It was almost as though the Too-Tall gang had been a virus and he'd gotten over them. And even better, he woke up with a really big idea.

It had begun to take shape when the cubs were running home the day before. It had been on his mind as he drifted off to sleep. Now it was fully formed. It was a way to get cubs not to start smoking and maybe even to get them to stop after they started.

He could hardly wait to tell his fellow scouts about it. He could have told Sister about it at breakfast. But he didn't. He decided to wait until the four of them were on their way to Ralph's houseboat.

But before he could get into his big idea, Fred had a question. "Do you think Ralph will want to help Dr. Gert put on her health rally?" he asked.

"We'll find out about that soon enough," said Brother. "But first I gotta tell you this idea I had. It's just what Dr. Gert is looking for. It's an idea about how to discourage cubs from smoking."

"Oh?" said Fred.

"Remember yesterday," said Brother, "when we were headed home and Sister yelled, 'Last one to Eagle Road is a rotten egg!'?"

"Sure," said Sister. "I got there first, and you were the rotten egg."

"Well, that's my idea," said Brother.

Sister, Fred, and Lizzy looked puzzled.

"Don't you get it?" said Brother.

Puzzlement gave way to bafflement.

"It's so simple!" said Brother. "*Nobody wants to be a rotten egg!* Everybody wants to win! Everybody wants to be first. First across the goal line, first around the track, first driving for the basket, first down the soccer field!"

"I get it," said Fred. "And if they smoke, they're not going to be first. They're gonna be an out-of-breath, short-of-wind rotten egg."

"Exactly!" said Brother.

"Yes," said Sister. "But how do we get that across?"

"Easy," said Brother. "Instead of putting on a health rally, Dr. Gert puts on a health rally *and* fitness field day!"

"Hey! A field day!" said Lizzy.

"With all kinds of races!" said Sister.

"Wind sprints, dashes, hurdles, the mile!" said Fred. "There'll be plenty of room for it on that big field next to the hospital!"

"Well," said Brother, after a pause. "What do you think of my idea?"

"*Your* idea? *Your* idea?" said Sister. "*I'm* the one who said 'Last one to Eagle Road is a rotten egg!'"

Brother started to argue but caught himself when he realized that Sister was just kidding. Besides, Ralph's houseboat was just ahead.

Ralph's place was just as messy as ever — maybe even messier. There was mold on the hull, the brightwork was the color of lead, and pond scum was creeping up the gangplank.

"Do you really think Ralph will agree to help Dr. Gert with the health rally?" asked Fred.

"You never know with Ralph," said Brother. "Just when you're convinced he's the worst guy in the world, he'll do something really nice!"

The scouts pressed forward along the overgrown path.

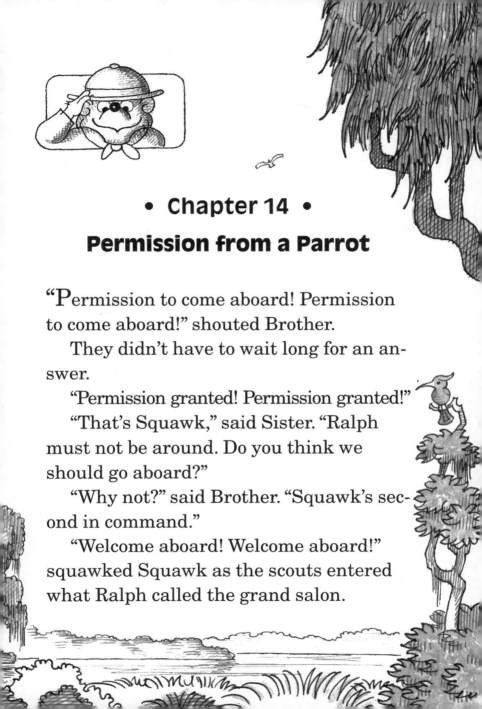

• Chapter 14 •

Permission from a Parrot

"Permission to come aboard! Permission to come aboard!" shouted Brother.

They didn't have to wait long for an answer.

"Permission granted! Permission granted!"

"That's Squawk," said Sister. "Ralph must not be around. Do you think we should go aboard?"

"Why not?" said Brother. "Squawk's second in command."

"Welcome aboard! Welcome aboard!" squawked Squawk as the scouts entered what Ralph called the grand salon.

Grand mess would have been more accurate. Not that it couldn't have been fixed up nicely. There was a big easy chair with a side table in the center of the large low-ceilinged room. A little galley and a breakfast nook were squeezed in at the back of the room. A shelf followed the big curved windows that formed the front of the main cabin. Ralph used part of the shelf as an office. Along with a typewriter and piles of crumpled paper, there was a big yellow pad with writing on it. Brother looked at it, thinking it might be a "be back soon" note. But it wasn't. It was a "things to do" note. This is what it said:

THINGS TO DO
1. Arrange for rock concert.
2. Inspect sample jackets.
3. Pick up tickets at Fastprint.
4. Contact Beartown Outdoor Advertising about Project X.

Rock concert? Jackets? Tickets? Project X? What was it all about? That's the way it was with Ralph. There were always more questions than answers. You never quite knew what he was up to until your watch was gone or you'd signed up for twenty years of a magazine you'd never heard of.

While Brother was trying to puzzle out Ralph's "things to do" note, Sister said, "What do you make of this?" She was talking about an easel that had been set up in the main cabin. On it was a large display book — the kind lecturers use.

"Maybe Ralph's going to lecture Squawk on how to be a crook and a swindler," said Lizzy.

"How about checking it out," said Fred. "It can't hurt to know what Ralph's up to."

"Do you really think we should?" said Lizzy.

"Be my guest! Be my guest!" squawked Squawk.

"Thank you, Squawk," said Brother. But when he looked at the first page he was just as puzzled as he was by the "things to do" note.

"'Excitement! Adventure! Sophistication!'" said Fred, reading the three words that were printed on the page in big block letters. The next page showed a moose standing in a pond.

"I recognize that moose from somewhere," said Sister.

"Sure you do," said Fred. "You recognize it from the Moose Cigarette package. It's on billboards all over town."

Brother turned to the picture of Moe Moose on the next page.

"Oh, I like him much better," said Lizzy.

"Yeah," agreed Sister. "He's really cool."

"And look!" said Lizzy as Brother turned the pages. "Moe Moose jackets, Moe Moose caps, Moe Moose everything."

Brother was beginning to figure out what Ralph was up to. The pieces of the

puzzle were beginning to fall into place: the items on the "things to do" list, the moose in the pond, the new supercool Moe Moose character, the jackets, the caps.

"Notice anything odd about this Moe Moose character?" asked Brother.

"Yeah," said Sister. "In every picture he's smoking."

"What's going on?" said Lizzy. "What's it all mean?"

"It means," said Brother, "that there's no way Ralph is going to help Dr. Gert with the antismoking health rally. Because," Brother continued, *"he's working for the Moose Tobacco Company!"*

"Why, that's awful!" said Lizzy.

"It looks like they're *trying* to get kids to smoke," said Sister.

"Isn't that illegal?" said Lizzy.

"It's illegal to *sell* cigarettes to cubs," said Fred. "But it's not illegal to do stuff that makes smoking seem cool and exciting. You heard what Chief Bruno said. It's called 'freedom of speech.'"

"Oh yeah?" said Sister. "Well, we have freedom of speech, too, and —"

"Speaking of cool," said Brother, "let's cool it. Because here comes Ralph!"

They closed the display book and made sure the "things to do" note didn't look disturbed. All they could do now was hope that Squawk didn't give them away.

• Chapter 15 •

Ralph's Big Event

"Ah! My very good friends, the Bear Scouts!" said Ralph when he saw his visitors. "What a lovely surprise. To what do I owe this pleasure?"

"Er, we just happened to be in the neighborhood," said Brother, "and thought we'd stop by."

"Whatever the reason, I'm delighted to see you," said Ralph, "because I've got something truly wonderful coming up. My friends, I'm putting on the biggest rock rally in the history of Bear Country. Featuring those rat stars, Too-Tall and the Gang."

"I think you mean 'rap stars,'" said Sister.

"What's the difference? As long as it's groovy," said Ralph.

He reached down, switched on the radio, and twiddled the dial. The scouts listened as the sound came up. It was the Too-Tall gang singing on the radio:

All make way,
This means you,
The Too-Tall gang
Is comin' Through.

So look out
All you dweebs and drips
we're the Four Bad
Bears
of the Apocalypse
All make way . . .

"How about that," said Fred.

"I heard they might cut a record," said Brother. Even though he had been with them just yesterday, they seemed like voices from a forgotten past.

"Exactly," said Ralph. "And it's going to get plenty of airtime before my big event."

"Tell us more about this event," said Brother.

"It's going to be fabulous," said Ralph. "My gift to the youth of Bear Country. We're taking over the old closed-down drive-in movie theater. Too-Tall and the Gang will be our main attraction. There'll be hundreds of door prizes: jackets, vests, backpacks, free caps for everyone . . ."

Moe Moose jackets, *Moe Moose* vests, *Moe Moose* backpacks, *Moe Moose* caps, thought Brother as Ralph raved on.

"And the fabulous, unbelievable Project X, an attraction worthy to be called the Eighth Wonder of the World!"

Hmm, thought Brother. There's that Project X again.

"And just to be sure that you don't miss it, my friends," continued Ralph, "here are four front-row tickets . . . oops! There goes the phone."

"Thanks, Ralph," said Brother as Ralph went to answer the phone.

The scouts figured it was time to leave. They had some serious thinking to do. Not only had they failed to get Ralph's help with Dr. Gert's antismoking health rally, but they would be going up against Ralph's fabulous rock rally at the old drive-in, which was right next to the hospital field. And according to the tickets, both rallies were scheduled for the same weekend.

Ralph was well into his phone conversation as the scouts let themselves out.

"I don't care how much it costs," Ralph was saying. "Project X must be kept absolutely secret until the unveiling. Build it under a tent if you have to . . ."

Hmm, thought Brother, Project X again, as the scouts went down the gangplank.

• Chapter 16 •

Dangerous Game

"You were right about Ralph," said Fred. "Only you had it backwards: just when you think Ralph might do something nice, he turns out to be the worst guy in the world."

"Yeah," said Brother with a sigh. "I guess it's pretty hard to change the habits of a lifetime."

"The *bad* habits of a lifetime," added Sister.

The scouts were pretty glum as they came out of the woods that bordered the river where Ralph's houseboat was moored. Now that they were out of the woods and in open country, they started to sort things out.

"How about how Ralph's big rock rally is going to be on the same weekend as Dr. Gert's big health rally," said Fred.

"I've been thinking about that," said Brother.

"And how about how it's going to be at the old closed-down drive-in that's right next to the hospital field," said Lizzy.

"I've been thinking about that, too," said Brother.

"Maybe Dr. Gert should move her health rally to a different weekend," said Fred.

"I've been thinking about that, too," said Brother.

"Boy!" said Sister, who hadn't completely forgiven Brother for his Too-Tall adventure. "Listen to the big thinker! It looks to me like it's time to stop thinking and *do* something!"

"I've been thinking about that, too," said Brother. "Well, see you guys later. There's something I gotta do." With that, Brother parted company with the troop.

Brother had an idea about how to deal with all the problems his fellow scouts had raised. It was a long shot and a risky one at that. But Brother decided it was worth a try.

His fellow scouts were absolutely right: going head-to-head against Ralph Ripoff's rock rally would be suicidal. How could Dr. Gert's antismoking health rally compete against Moe Moose? With their new hit rap record, the Too-Tall gang alone could swamp the health rally. *Unless Brother's idea for interfering with Ralph's rock rally worked.*

But it was going to be scary. Because it meant going back into the Too-Tall gang's dangerous den. He knew the gang would be furious with him for standing them up.

Nobody stood up the Too-Tall gang and got away with it. The thing Brother was counting on to protect him was basketball. Brother was a wizard basketball player, and Too-Tall couldn't turn down a good game.

Brother took a deep breath and stepped out of the woods onto the stretch of black-top the gang used as a basketball court.

Too-Tall was practicing jumpers. The gang was nowhere in sight. Brother thought he heard music. They must be in the clubhouse listening to their new record.

KEEP OUT!

Too-Tall knew Brother was there, but he didn't say a word.

"Hi, Too-Tall," said Brother.

"You made me look bad yesterday when you didn't come back," said Too-Tall.

"Sorry about that," said Brother.

"You made me look real bad," said Too-Tall.

"I said I was sorry," said Brother.

"Maybe you'd better get outta here before I turn the gang loose on you," said Too-Tall.

"Hey," said Brother. "Just because I'm not going to be in the gang doesn't mean we can't play a little hoops."

Too-Tall didn't say anything. He just kept on shooting jumpers. Brother figured he was deciding between playing some hoops and turning the gang loose on him. Brother held his breath.

Finally Too-Tall tossed his cigarette away and shouted, "Hey, gang! Get out here! We're gonna play some hoops!"

Vinnie, Skuzz, and Smirk poured out of the clubhouse in a cloud of smoke. They surrounded Brother. "Let's give it to him," said Skuzz.

"I said we're gonna play some hoops," said Too-Tall.

"At least let us pants him," said Vinnie.

Brother felt a chill. He could see himself running away with the wind blowing through his shorts.

"Me and Goody Two-shoes against you three," ordered Too-Tall. "We'll play half-court."

"Why half-court?" said Brother. "Why is it always half-court? What's the matter with full-court? Can't you smokers handle full-court?"

Too-Tall glared at Brother. "Okay, Mr. Bear Scout. Full-court."

There followed a terrific hard-fought game. Back and forth, back and forth they ran, the full length of the court. Again and again and again.

Brother and Too-Tall were leading
eighteen to ten when Vinnie croaked,
"Time-out!" and the whole gang, including
Too-Tall, collapsed, gasping for breath.
Brother rubbed it in as the gang lay there
choking and wheezing and blue in the face
by dribbling around and taking shots.

"You know something?" said Brother.
"You guys oughta be able to figure it out:
Basketball and smoking don't mix," he

YOU OUGHTA THINK
ABOUT SOMETHING THAT
TAKES LESS WIND— LIKE
TIDDLYWINKS OR TICKTACKTOE.

taunted. "You oughta think about something that takes less wind — like tiddlywinks or ticktacktoe."

Brother wasn't being all that brave. There was no way the gang could come after him. They were totally wiped out.

"Oh, yeah?" gasped Too-Tall. "Me and the gang can beat you and your creepy scout troop at anything, anytime, anywhere!"

"That sounds like a challenge to a duel," said Brother.

"Darn right!" snarled Too-Tall. "Do you accept?"

"I'll think about it and get back to you," said Brother.

With Too-Tall and the others beginning to catch their breath, Brother thought it best to skedaddle.

So he skedaddled.

• Chapter 17 •

A Lot to Tell

"Tiddlywinks or ticktacktoe?" said Sister. "You actually said that to Too-Tall?"

"Wow!" said Lizzy.

"You were lucky to escape with your life!" said Fred.

"Maybe so," said Brother. "But escape I did. And now we've got at least a fighting chance to win the battle of the dueling rallies. And," he added, "win it with a duel!"

"They actually challenged you to a duel?" said Fred.

"That's my story, and they're stuck with it," said Brother with a big grin. "Anyway, we've got a lot to tell Dr. Gert about."

"We have her home phone number," said Sister. "Let's give her a call."

So the scouts called up Dr. Gert and told her that her consultants were ready to consult. A meeting was arranged for the next day at the hospital.

Once again the Bear Scouts were climbing the front steps of the hospital for a meeting with Dr. Gert. As they climbed, they saw that a team of workbears was starting to get the hospital field ready for the big antismoking health rally. They also saw that across the way a bigger team of workbears was getting the old drive-in ready for Ralph's big rock rally.

But what the heck was going on with the huge drive-in movie screen? The whole thing was covered with a sort of tent, and workers were going in and out of it.

"What do you suppose?" said Lizzy.

"I don't know," said Brother. "It must be that Project X Ralph was talking about."

"Maybe it's going to be one of those big

projection screens they have at rock concerts," said Fred. "You know — where they
blow the rock stars up to fifty feet high."

"A fifty-foot-tall Too-Tall!" said Brother.
"That's *really* scary. Come on, scouts.
We've got a meeting to attend."

A quick elevator ride later, the scouts
were ushered into a conference room
where Dr. Gert and Scout Leader Jane
were waiting. Miss Stickler was there, too.
Miss Stickler, who was a stickler about being organized, was busy keeping things organized on her laptop computer.

"Greetings, scouts," said Dr. Gert. "We've been looking forward to your report."

"We have, too," said Brother. "But there's so much to tell that I hardly know where to start."

"There's so much bad news," Fred whispered to Brother. "Why don't you start with the good news: your fitness field-day idea?"

Dr. Gert and Scout Leader Jane listened, and Miss Stickler pecked away at her laptop as Brother explained his fitness field-day idea and why he thought it might help with the problem of cubs and smoking.

"Hmm," said Dr. Gert. "As you point out, nobody wants to be a rotten egg. Your point being that instead of threats and warnings about the future, we give cubs something of value *today*."

"Exactly," said Brother.

"Excuse me," said Miss Stickler, looking

up from her laptop. "But what *are* we giving them today?"

"We are giving them the breath of life," said Dr. Gert. "We are giving them the chance to have great healthy lungs and run like the wind. And all they have to do is stop smoking or not start."

"That's all very well," said Miss Stickler, reaching into her briefcase. "But take a look at what the other side is giving them."

"What other side?" asked Dr. Gert.

"This other side," said Miss Stickler, handing Dr. Gert a flier.

"What's this?" said Dr. Gert.

"It's just what it looks like," said Miss Stickler. "It's a flier for a huge prosmoking rally being put on by the Moose Tobacco Company. And it's going to take place right across from our rally and on the same weekend!"

"My goodness," said Dr. Gert as she

read the flier. " "The Moose Company presents Rock-and-Roll Party Time! . . . Introducing Moe Moose, the coolest critter on the scene . . . featuring rap superstars Too-Tall and the Gang performing their Top Forty hit, "The Too-Tall Gang Is Comin' Through" . . . free Moe Moose caps, hundreds of door prizes . . . and don't miss Project X, the Eighth Wonder of the World!' "

"Where did you get this?" asked Dr. Gert.

"They're all over town!" said Miss Stickler. "But that's not the question. The question is: What are we going to *do* about it?"

Dr. Gert turned to the scouts. "What do you know about this?" she asked.

"We know everything about it," said Brother. He and the other scouts explained that Ralph Ripoff was behind the whole thing. They told how they'd gone to ask Ralph to help with the health rally and discovered that he'd already sold out to the Moose Tobacco Company.

Scout Leader Jane was looking at the flier. "How are we going to compete with this?" she said.

"It'll be a battle of the dueling rallies, all right," said Brother. "But I think we have an idea how to deal with it."

"I have an idea, too," said Miss Stickler. "We'll fight 'em at every turn! I'll chain myself to every cigarette machine in Bear Country!"

"Simultaneously or one at a time?" said Dr. Gert. "Look, Sally. We all know how

I'LL CHAIN MYSELF TO EVERY CIGARETTE MACHINE IN BEAR COUNTRY!

you feel. We agree with you. But our job is to protect youth against the evils of smoking. Not to make a big fuss and end up in jail. Because that's where you'll end up if you start chaining yourself to cigarette machines. All right then, Brother. You said you had an idea how to cope with this prosmoking rock rally. We're listening."

Brother began by telling about his visit to the Too-Tall gang's hideout to play basketball. "You see," he said, "I knew that if I could talk them into playing full-court —"

That's when Scout Leader Jane shouted, "Good grief! Would you look at that!" She was looking out the window.

All present rushed to the window, which had a full view of the old drive-in across the way. The workbears had taken the cover off the huge drive-in movie screen.

The scouts had been wrong about it being made into a projection screen. It was something much more shocking. It was a billboard. The biggest the scouts had ever seen. On it was a picture of that cool critter, Moe Moose. He was wearing a cool cap nestled between his antlers, a purple turtleneck, an orange jacket, a diamond stud in one ear, *and he was blowing smoke rings*. Real smoke rings. They came out of his mouth one after the other in tight little O's, then grew bigger and bigger as they billowed out over Beartown.

Dr. Gert, Miss Stickler, Scout Leader Jane, and the scouts were speechless. Except for Sister.

"You know something," she said. "I think it *is* the Eighth Wonder of the World."

• Chapter 18 •
Take That, Moe Moose!

Some of those present were so shaken by the idea of going head-to-head against Ralph's rally that they wanted to postpone the antismoking health rally to another weekend.

But Dr. Gert wouldn't hear of it. "No!" she said. "This is important! We can't give in to the tobacco interests. We've got to go head-to-head against them. We've got to show them up for what they are: folks who are trying to addict cubs to smoking!"

Once it was decided to meet Moe Moose head-on, the rally began to take shape.

Everybody pitched in. Miss Stickler kept things organized on her handy-dandy laptop. Scout Leader Jane, who'd had practice writing slogans when she ran for mayor, came up with a pretty cool slogan for the antismoking rally. It said, "Start smoking and you've lost the race before it starts." The Bear Scouts were put in charge of planning the fitness field day.

And while Dr. Gert may not have known much about putting on shows when she started, going up against Ralph was a crash course in showmanship. First, with the help of Miss Stickler and the Bear Scouts, she worked out a plan of attack.

If Ralph's prosmoking rally was going to give away caps, then the antismoking rally would give away caps. But caps cost money. Moose Tobacco had a tankful of money. Beartown Hospital was running on empty. Where would the caps come from?

How about Highway Hat, out on the highway? Highway Hat would probably be
glad to donate caps. But how many? And
"how many" wasn't the only problem.
Highways Hat's caps were plain. Ralph's
caps had Moe Moose logos on them. The
antismoking rally's caps needed a logo.
Hey, the rally could have a logo contest!

How about door prizes? If Ralph's rally
was going to give away door prizes, then
the antismoking rally would give away
door prizes. But where would the money
come from? How about Squire Grizzly?
What was the good of having the richest
bear in Bear Country on your board of di-
rectors if you couldn't hit him up for door
prizes?

And, of course, every door prize would
have the new antismoking logo on it. Take
that, Moe Moose!

How about a loudspeaker system? Dr.
Gert could put in a call to Beartown

Sound, the company that serviced the hospital's intercom, and tell them that a loudspeaker system was needed for Beartown Hospital's Antismoking Health Rally and Fitness Field Day.

Hey, that was an awful mouthful. A better name was needed. Something short, something catchy. How about another contest?

And what about the field? Who was setting it up for the big field day? The Bear Scouts were in charge. They could run like the wind, but they didn't know beans about how to set up for a field day. Dr. Gert would have to get in touch with Coach Grizzmeyer over at the school. He was an expert. And when he said "Jump," everybody said "How high?"

Dr. Gert put her plan into action right away. First she held the logo contest. The winner was a fantastic logo showing a death's head with cigarette crossbones in

a circle with a line through it. Then she lined up donations: a loudspeaker system from Beartown Sound, money for door prizes from Squire Grizzly, and caps with the new logo on them from Highway Hat. Next, she held the contest to find a new name for the rally. *And the winner was . . .*

It was short, it was catchy! And things that ended with "orama" were always successful.

Finally, Dr. Gert contacted Coach Grizzmeyer, who agreed to help. The coach was a tiger. Before you could say "Take twenty laps," the field had a long-jump pit, a high-jump site, a pole-vault place, and a half-mile track.

Somehow, some way, the job got done. The field was ready. The big tent for the medical tests was ready. The doctors and nurses who would do the tests were ready. It was a kind of miracle.

But it wasn't the only miracle in town. Ralph Ripoff had performed a miracle of his own just across the way. The old drive-in had been transformed. It was festooned with banners and bunting. The old admission booth had been converted into Moe Moose headquarters. There were cutouts of Moe Moose on every one of the poles that used to connect the cars to the sound system. Moe Moose was everywhere. And everywhere he was, he was smoking a cigarette. And in the really big picture on the giant billboard, the smoothest, coolest critter of them all was not only smoking a cigarette, he was blowing big, beautiful, billowing smoke rings.

The smoke rings made Miss Stickler,

who was a stickler for clean air, furious. She called the mayor's office but didn't get past the mayor's secretary. Which wasn't a surprise. It was well known that Ralph and the mayor were buddies. So she called the Air Quality Control Board in Big Bear City. They said they would look into it. But that would take forever.

Tired but hopeful, the Bear Scouts were going down the hospital steps after a final report to Dr. Gert. Both rallies would open the next day. Healthorama would go head-to-head against Ralph's rock rally, featuring Too-Tall and the Gang. The battle of the dueling rallies would finally happen. And that wouldn't be the only duel. At least not if Brother's plan worked.

"Isn't that Miss Stickler's van parked in front of the hospital?" said Fred.

The scouts strolled over to the van. "Hi, Miss Stickler," said Brother. "What are you doing?"

"Working on my laptop," said Miss Stickler. "I've got it hooked up to a modem connected to my car phone. I'm trying to tap into the computer that works that disgusting billboard."

"Why are you doing that?" asked Fred.

"Because," said Miss Stickler, pecking furiously at her laptop, "any computer that can be programmed can be deprogrammed."

As the scouts headed home, Brother said, "At least she's not chaining herself to any cigarette machines."

• Chapter 19 •

Rally versus Rally

Healthorama kicked off at twelve noon sharp. Since Ralph's rally wasn't scheduled to start until two o'clock, Dr. Gert's antismoking rally wouldn't have any competition for two hours.

The early crowds were encouraging. Lots of grown-ups were moving through the medical tents getting their blood pressure checked and their fitness level tested. All three treadmills were in use. Dr. Gert was doing a slide lecture based on her Horrors of Smoking exhibition.

The crowds were even bigger outside the tent. Cubs were lined up for every event; the free caps and the door prizes were a huge hit. The antismoking death's head logo was pronounced cool. Coach Grizzmeyer stood on a platform at the center of the field directing the action over the loudspeaker system.

With things going smoothly inside the tent, Dr. Gert had come out to watch the field-day action. "Do you think we're getting our antismoking message across to the cubs?" she asked.

"No question about it," said Brother. "If all that running and jumping doesn't do it, that logo will."

The message of the death's head logo was certainly clear. Not only was it on every cap and door prize, there were blowups of it posted all over the field.

It was almost two o'clock, the time when Ralph's Rock-and-Roll Party Time was scheduled to start. Scouts Sister, Fred, and Lizzy, who had fanned out checking the events, rejoined Brother and

Dr. Gert. They all knew that Ralph was a genius at putting on a show, so they couldn't help being a little worried about the competition. But as they looked across the way at the drive-in, it was beginning to seem that perhaps Ralph's genius had deserted him.

The drive-in looked fine all dressed up with banners and bunting. A stage had been built at the foot of the billboard. And, of course, the giant Moe Moose billboard was blowing its smoke rings. But that was it. There was no one there. No one had shown up.

But then they heard the distant music and knew right away that Ralph had not only not lost his genius, but was about to make the grandest grand entrance in the history of Bear Country.

The first thing they saw was a dancing, prancing, thirty-foot-tall Moe Moose on stilts, smoking a three-foot-long cigarette.

Strutting around him was Ralph himself, twirling his cane like a baton. Behind them was a brass band all decked out in the Moe Moose colors of purple and orange. Behind the band, the Too-Tall gang was waving from a float that was a replica of the gang's rusty car parts clubhouse. And behind *that* . . . cubs as far as the eye could see.

"How discouraging," said Dr. Gert. "It's the Pied Piper all over again. Only this time he's leading cubs to the death and disease caused by smoking."

With Moe Moose and Ralph leading the way, the parade of cubs flowed into the drive-in and gathered around the stage at the foot of the great Moe Moose billboard. That's when it got *really* discouraging. The field-day cubs stopped running and jumping and, almost as one, swarmed over to the drive-in.

Dr. Gert sighed. "You told me he was a genius," she said.

"We're not dead yet," said Brother. "Follow me, scouts!"

The troop ran across the nearly empty field and climbed onto Coach Grizzmeyer's platform.

"Excuse us, coach!" said Brother. "Would you please lower the microphone? We're taking over."

• Chapter 20 •
Showdown

Rap stars Too-Tall and the Gang were to be first on the program, and the crowd was clamoring for them to start. Too-Tall, Skuzz, Vinnie, and Smirk had boxes of Moe Moose hats, jackets, and vests and were running about the stage tossing them to the crowd.

Ralph tested the loudspeaker system by tapping the microphone. "Testing. One, two. Testing. One, two."

The crowd quieted down. But before Ralph could begin, another loudspeaker and another voice took over. It was the voice of Brother Bear speaking from the hospital field.

"ATTENTION, PLEASE! ATTENTION, PLEASE! THE BEAR SCOUTS CALLING TOO-TALL AND THE GANG!"

All eyes turned to Healthorama. The scouts had gotten Too-Tall's attention, all right, and the attention of everyone in the crowd. And especially that of Ralph Ripoff.

"YOU CHALLENGED US TO A DUEL! WE ACCEPT THE CHALLENGE!"

"Don't listen to him!" cried Ralph.

But Too-Tall was listening, and so was everyone in the crowd.

"AND SINCE YOU MADE THE CHALLENGE, WE GET TO CHOOSE THE WEAPON!"

"Start the music! Start the music!" begged Ralph.

"AND THE WEAPON WE CHOOSE IS THE 880 RELAY RACE! FOUR AGAINST FOUR! THE BREATH-OF-LIFE BEAR

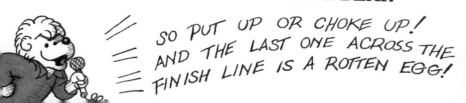

SO PUT UP OR CHOKE UP! AND THE LAST ONE ACROSS THE FINISH LINE IS A ROTTEN EGG!

SCOUTS AGAINST THE SMOKING, CHOKING TOO-TALL GANG!"

"*Please* don't listen to them!" begged Ralph.

"SO PUT UP OR CHOKE UP! AND THE LAST ONE ACROSS THE FINISH LINE IS A ROTTEN EGG!"

Too-Tall was in a fury. He grabbed the microphone away from Ralph. "YOU'RE ON! YOU GOODY TWO-SHOES LITTLE BEAR SCOUT CREEPS! YOU'RE ON!"

With that, Too-Tall and the Gang leaped down from the stage, cut through the crowd, and reported to Coach Grizzmeyer at the hospital field. The crowd surged after them. The scouts were already spaced out along the track, with Brother far down the track in the anchor position.

"All right," said Coach Grizzmeyer. "Here's how a relay race works."

"We know how a relay race works!" snarled Too-Tall. "Let's get on with it!"

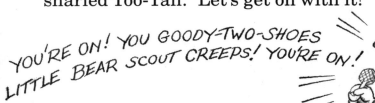

YOU'RE ON! YOU GOODY-TWO-SHOES LITTLE BEAR SCOUT CREEPS! YOU'RE ON!

"Who's running anchor?" asked the coach.

"I am, of course," said Too-Tall.

"Then take your positions," said Coach Grizzmeyer.

The crowd was silent as the gang took their positions. The suspense mounted. It would be Fred against Skuzz, Sister against Vinnie, Lizzy against Smirk, and Brother against Too-Tall.

Coach Grizzmeyer gave Fred and Skuzz the batons they would be handing off, raised the starting gun, and . . .

BANG!

Off they went down the track, knees pumping, feet pounding, lungs . . . Did somebody mention lungs? Well, lungs were what it was all about. The Breath-of-Life Scouts' lungs were in tip-top shape. The smoking, choking Too-Tall gang's lungs were not. So it was really no contest. The Too-Tall gang didn't win a single leg of the relay race.

Brother crossed the finish line, baton held high! Sister, Fred, and Lizzy joined him there. "Slogan time!" said Brother. They all grasped the baton and shouted, "One for all and all for one!"

They hardly heard themselves, so great was the roar of the crowd. Before they knew what was happening they were hoisted onto the shoulders of celebrating cubs. Caps were thrown in the air. Lots of Moe Moose caps were thrown away and exchanged for antismoking hats. Moe Moose jackets and vests were thrown in the trash.

What about the gasping, wheezing, choking Too-Tall gang? They had collapsed along the track, where they were being given oxygen by teams of doctors and nurses.

• Chapter 21 •

Up in Smoke

Ralph had watched the whole disaster
unfold from the stage at the foot of the
Moe Moose billboard. He knew it was over
when he saw stretcher bearers take the
Too-Tall gang into the hospital emergency
room. And just when he thought things
couldn't get any worse, they got worse.

Throughout the whole disaster, Moe
Moose kept right on blowing his big beautiful smoke rings, one big round O after
another. But now the sound of the
computer-controlled machinery behind
the billboard was changing. It had a different rhythm. It had speeded up.

Ralph looked up. He couldn't understand what he was seeing. Moe Moose was no longer blowing O's. It was hard to tell from below, but Ralph thought he saw an S . . . and then an M . . . and then . . .

Across the way, Miss Stickler sat in her van looking at the billboard with deep satisfaction. Others were, too. Including the Bear Scouts.

"Hey, look!" said Fred. "No more smoke rings! There's an S . . . and an M . . . and an O . . ."

"Unless I miss my guess," said Brother, "Moe Moose is going to spell 'Smoking kills! Smoking kills!'"

"You're right!" said Sister. "There's a K . . . and an I."

"I suppose you've noticed," said Fred. "There's Miss Stickler in her van pounding away at her laptop."

"Look," said Brother. "Ralph's climbing up behind the billboard. He's going to try to stop the machinery!"

"Wow!" said Fred. "He stopped it, all
right! Look at that!"

Black smoke was pouring out of the
billboard. Before you could say "Moe
Moose," the entire Eighth Wonder of the
World was hidden in a cloud of thick black
smoke. When the smoke cleared, Ralph
could be seen sitting at the edge of the
stage. He and his creation looked as if a
vacuum cleaner had blown up in their
faces.

The scouts walked over to Miss Stickler's van. "Was that some of your work?" asked Brother.

"I have nothing to say on the matter," said Miss Stickler. "Except to enlarge on what I said earlier: Any computer that can be programmed can be deprogrammed. And *re*programmed."

The scouts headed back to the field, where Healthorama was still going strong.

"Do you think Too-Tall and his gang will stop smoking?" asked Lizzy.

"They might," said Brother. "But according to Dr. Gert, it's hard to stop once you start."

"But," said Fred, "she also says that if you stop soon enough, your lungs will come back pretty strong."

"If Too-Tall and his gang stop, they'll be able to run us into the ground," said Sister.

"That's life," said Brother.

115

• Chapter 22 •

A Place of Honor

The Moe Moose rock rally was canceled. Healthorama, however, ran the whole weekend. While there was no way to tell for sure how many cubs were persuaded to stop smoking or not to start, lots of cubs kept wearing their antismoking caps and jackets long after Healthorama. And that was a good sign.

The Bear Scouts got their official Public Health Merit Badge, and it looked fine on display in the clubhouse. But it had to share the honor with an *un*official Public Health Merit Badge that looked like this:

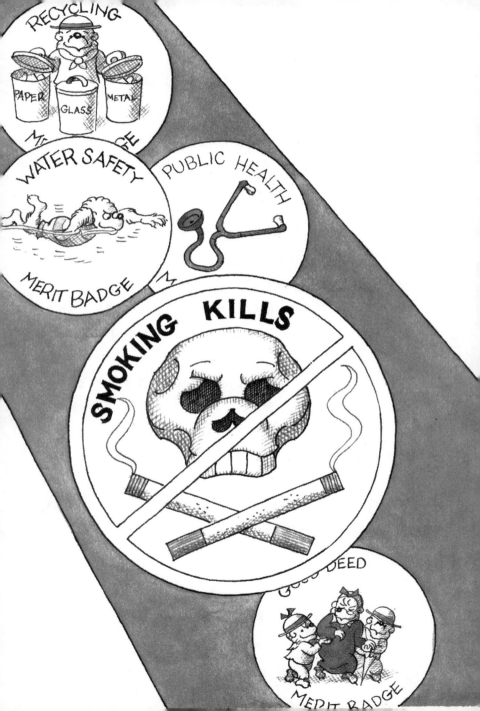

• About the Authors •

Stan and Jan Berenstain have been writing and illustrating books about bears for more than thirty years. Their very first book about the Bear Scout characters was published in 1967. Through the years the Bear Scouts have done their best to defend the weak, catch the crooked, joust against the unjust, and rally against rottenness of all kinds. In fact, the scouts have done such a great job of living up to the Bear Scout Oath, the authors say, that "they deserve a series of their own."

Stan and Jan Berenstain live in Bucks County, Pennsylvania. They have two sons, Michael and Leo, and four grandchildren. Michael is an artist, and Leo is a writer. Michael did the pictures in this book.

Message from the New York State Commissioner of Health

Children are New York State's greatest resource. As parents and guardians, you are concerned for your children's health and safety as well as for their future successes. Protect your children's health by keeping them away from secondhand smoke and informing them about the dangers of smoking. Nurture their interests and sense of security by taking time to read with them. Reading together is an important way to make sure your child understands how to stay healthy. Reading is also an important building block for future success. Together we can make a difference in every child's life.

Antonia C. Novell, m.d. m.p.h. Dr. P.H.

Antonia C. Novello, M.D., M.P.H., Dr.P.H.
New York State Commissioner of Health

*The best way to protect your children is to quit smoking...
call New York State's Quitline at 1-888-609-6292.*

Build a Healthy Future for New York State's Second-Graders

As a parent or guardian of a second-grader, you're building the foundation for your child's future success. Two important parts of that foundation are good health and literacy. Like parents and guardians everywhere, you are encouraging your second-grader to master reading and writing skills, and at the same time you are modeling good health habits.

Second grade is a good time for you and your child to read about and discuss health issues such as the fact that breathing other people's smoke hurts them. Second-graders are beginning to read for information at the same time that they are developing an awareness of themselves and their bodies. Reading *The Berenstain Bear Scouts and the Sinister Smoke Ring* with your child will increase your child's understanding of the dangers of smoking and secondhand smoke. It will build your child's communication skills at the same time.

On page 2 of these Parent/Guardian Pages you'll find information and suggestions for keeping your child's world smoke-free. On page 3 you'll find a story summary and a list of the key messages in the Berenstain Bears book. On pages 3 and 4 you'll find reasons for reading aloud with your child and ideas for building reading skills. "Laying the Foundation for Your Child's Future," on page 5, summarizes the benefits of reading together and keeping your child's environment smoke-free.

Secondhand Smoke: Facts and Risks

- Tobacco use is the leading preventable cause of death in the United States.[1]
- Tobacco use causes more than 430,000 deaths per year from diseases such as heart disease, lung cancer, and emphysema.[2]
- Exposure to secondhand tobacco smoke causes an additional 53,000 deaths per year from heart disease, lung cancer, and other diseases among nonsmokers.[3]
- Even very short-term exposures to secondhand smoke have major impacts on the heart and blood.[4]
- Since 1991, there has been a reduction in exposure of the U.S. population to secondhand tobacco smoke. However, more than half of American youth continue to be exposed to this known powerful toxin.[5]
- Over 4,000 different chemicals have been identified in secondhand smoke, and several of these chemicals cause cancer.[6]

Breathing secondhand smoke can be harmful to children's health. The U.S. Environmental Protection Agency (EPA) has found that children who breathe secondhand smoke are more likely to suffer from:

- Bronchitis and pneumonia
- More ear infections
- Wheezing and coughing spells
- More frequent and severe asthma attacks[7]

The National Cancer Institute links secondhand smoke and

- Sudden Infant Death Syndrome (SIDS)
- New cases of childhood asthma[8]

You can protect your children from secondhand smoke by taking these steps:
- Keep your home smoke-free. Choose not to smoke in your home and do not permit others to do so.
- Choose not to smoke around children, especially infants and toddlers. Do not permit babysitters or others who work in your home to smoke in the house or near young children.
- Make sure your children are not exposed to tobacco smoke at school, pre-school, or daycare, or in cars with other adults.[9]

Sources: 1. National Center for Environmental Health, "One Page Summary, National Report on Human Exposure to Environmental Chemicals," March 2001 [www.cdc.gov/nceh/dls/tobaccou.htm]; 2. National Center for Chronic Disease Prevention and Health Promotion Web Site, "Risk Behaviors/Tobacco Use," (updated 7/23/01) [www.cdc.gov/nccdphp/tobacco.htm]; 3. SA Glantz and WW Parmley, "Passive smoking and heart disease. Epidemiology, physiology, and biochemistry," Circulation. 1991; 83: 1-12; 4. Ryo Otsuka, et al., "Acute Effects of Passive Smoking on the Coronary Circulation in Young Adults," Journal of the American Medical Association. 2001; 286: 436-441. 5. National Center for Environmental Health Web Site, "Highlights, National Report on Human Exposure to Environmental Chemicals," March 2001 [www.cdc.gov/nceh/dls/report/Highlights.htm]; 6. U.S. Environmental Protection Agency, Office of Children's Health Protection, "Air They Breathe" Web site (updated 1/19/00) [www.epa.gov/children/air.htm]; 7., 8., 9. U.S. Environmental Protection Agency, "Secondhand Smoke" Web page, April 2000 [www.epa.gov/iaq/ets/smokefree.html].

Reading Makes the Difference

Reading the Story

When Brother Bear begins making friends and smoking cigarettes with the Too-Tall Gang, the other Bear Scouts call on Gramps for help. After Gramps warns Brother Bear of the dangers of smoking, the Bear Scouts plan a special trip to the Beartown Hospital to learn more about how smoking hurts your body. As a result, the Scouts plan an antismoking rally. At their "Healthorama," the Bears show everyone the unhealthy effects of smoking by challenging Too-Tall and his friends to a race that leaves the smokers gasping for breath.

Some Key Messages in the Story to Share with Your Child

- Smoking hurts your health. (Chapters 9, 11, 16, 20)
- You can make healthy choices. (Chapters 12, 13, 16, 19, 20)
- Tobacco companies try to make smoking look like fun, but it's really dangerous. (Chapters 10, 14, 15)
- Children and grown-ups can learn from each other. (Chapters 7, 8, 9, 10, 17, 18)
- True friends care about your health. (Chapters 3, 8, 9, 11)

Reading with Your Child

Researchers agree that reading aloud is the single best activity you can share with your child to insure his or her school success. Read on to discover more reasons why reading aloud is so important.

Six Great Reasons to Read Aloud

1. As you read aloud with your child, he or she is actively participating in the learning process. Reading aloud and creatively picturing the words you read strengthens your child's listening skills and expands his or her attention span.
2. Your child's reading comprehension level exceeds his or her reading ability level. You can read aloud from books that are above your child's own reading level, and he or she will still understand and enjoy the story.
3. When you read aloud, you model the rhythm of written language (which differs somewhat from the rhythm of spoken language).
4. Enjoying a good book together leads to exchanging ideas, thoughts, reactions, and opinions.
5. Children who are read to are motivated to read on their own.
6. Reading aloud helps your child compare and contrast books. With enough read-aloud experience, your child will develop tastes for particular book types and favorite authors and illustrators.

Tips on Building Reading Skills

Read together from *The Berenstain Bear Scouts and the Sinister Smoke Ring* and help your child develop important learning skills in the process. Here's how:

- **Engage in *shared reading*** by taking turns reading a page or two of the book with your child. (Shared reading provides a stepping-stone to reading independently.)

- **React to what you read.** (*"Wow! I'd be upset if someone like Too-Tall offered you a cigarette!"*) Then, invite your child to offer an opinion. (*"What do you think you would do?"*)

- **Strengthen prediction skills** by asking your child to tell what might come next in the story. Compare his or her prediction with what actually happens. (*"You thought Gramps would be mad at Brother Bear, but instead he told Brother about his own poor choices."*)

- **Target vocabulary skills** by skimming a passage you plan to read aloud, and talk together about any unfamiliar words. Keep a children's dictionary nearby so you can look the word up together and relate it to the book. (*"The Bear Scouts are having a rally—a large get-together—to get people excited about healthy choices."*)

- **Offer your child a *guided reading experience*** by playing games that call attention to spelling patterns, words, letters, sounds, etc. (*"Do you know a word that rhymes with Brother?"* or *"Can you find a word that ends in ing?"*) Ask your child's teacher for a list of phonetic skills your child is working on in school.

4